Runty's Adventure
A Story Of Love

by
Chaffee Castleton

CREDITS
Written by Chaffee Castleton
Edited by Julia & Barbara Wood
Design and Production by Mother Press www.motherpress.com
Art by Dana Queen www.danaqueen.com
Published by Julia J. Castleton

ISBN: 978-0-578-06109-2

printed in Hong Kong

Dear Mother,

   I'm having trouble writing this letter to you
because I'm in awe of you, still, even though
you are gone.
   Did you know you are my mentor as well
as my mommy? You are my spiritual and
creative mentor, always telling me to have
faith in myself and be adventurous—to risk
something in my life and go forward with
all of my heart and soul. You would tell me
to go out into the world with a heart full of
love and to be sure to write a little every day.
   We did it Mom! My gift to you is to share
your story with the world. I know that
everyone who reads this tale of Runty will
understand your message and become better
for this.

                         Your Daughter,
                         Julia

When I first read Chaffee Castleton's "Runty's Adventure" it served as my bedtime story. I kept it on my old mahogany night table by the reading lamp. The raw manuscript on plain 'white paper read as a wonderful poetic allegory.

Mrs. C's heart must have been beating as pure and wholesomely honest as her main character, Runty, as she wrote this love story for all ages. You will love both Chaffee and Runty by the time you have turned the last page.

It has been my supreme pleasure to work with Chaffee Castleton's daughter, Julia Grant Castleton. She beams with the light of her mother's soul. They are kindred spirits with an innocence only a few posses in our world of change and confusion.

These human elements and an intelligent, well-researched account of animal life on the African Serengheti create a compelling and educational story, with our fifty animals represented in the natural world and the laws that govern it.

The journey takes you from the forest, across the Serengheti, and on to the Indian Ocean. A geological adventure.

Thank you Julia. Thank you Chaffee. I feel enriched from this experience. Now we can share this long-overdue adventure for all ages with the rest of the world.

Enjoy!
Barbara Wood

To
Chaffee

Table of Contents

The Beginning

ot all of Africa is jungle. There is endless grazing land on the African veldt, the Serengeti. And deep forest lies at the base of snow topped mountains. In the forested slopes of Mount Kenya, at the equator, at the very heart of Africa, there grew a giant tree called a Symbawa. This tree plunged its roots deep into the earth. Its verdant top shook triumphantly with every passing tempest. Nothing could mar its beauty. In this majestic tree, which shelters much wild life, there lived a family of tree hyraxes. A hyrax is a big, intelligent rodent covered with soft, thick fur. It has tiny ears and eyes as bright as blackberries shining in the sun. This particular hyrax family had five youngsters who were lovingly guarded over by a pair of wise and knowing parents. Four of the babies were large for their age and raced up and down the Symbawa tree, chasing each other from dawn to dark.

The fifth baby was the smallest. So small that one would be inclined to overlook him.

The family affectionately called him Runty. He was the quiet one and seemed always to be thinking. This habit is exceedingly strange in young hyraxes. He was quiet. Pondering. He would crouch softly beside his active siblings. Even his parents were not able to comprehend this.

Had they the slightest inkling of what it was, it would have shocked them greatly.

The World

*A*nd so his parents, like other furry parents the world around, raised their babies in rain and sun by night and day. You may be sure they instructed them with sound advice based on their long experience in the wild wood. And the litter listened, all ten beady eyes glistening, all ten ears pricked forward to their parents' words. They were admonished not to wander far from the giant Symbawa tree, at least not until they were old enough to start families of their own. Then they would be big enough and wise enough to avoid the dangers of the unknown and fend for themselves successfully. Obedient to their parents, the four brothers and sisters were quite content to live, play, eat, and sleep in the branches and exposed roots of the giant Symbawa tree. Here life was safe. Here life was complete.

And so the hours passed interestingly enough. But not for Runty. The world tugged at him mightily. That great marvelous globe, hurling quietly, imperceptibly, and continuously through space, firmly and securely revolving in an endless sky, constantly shifting night and day, winter and summer; floating with tremendous speed through space—that fascinating sun-shot, cloud-shadowed, moon-dazzled, rain-washed, wind-embraced, star-pierced, storm-flecked, snow-cloaked, sweet-smelling world.

Deliciously it stretched out through the forest and beyond on all sides of Runty—that furry little dot with a loving heart. And so Runty responded. One feeling possessed him: to go and find that which he felt in his heart, that love he could not yet comprehend.

The Forest

*R*unty loved the forest. It held a magic that seemed to call him. He longed to travel, alone, to contemplate and know what his own adventurous pilgrimage would reveal. Thus, all too soon, his parents' pleas unavailing, Runty bid good-bye to his tearful family and set out on his journey. He carried nothing with him but a heart full of love. This propelled him as he rushed toward life. He set out through the deep, dark forest with that ponderous, fastidious determination, and his little hyrax gait so light and airy a tread that it left no footprint on the rich loam of the forest floor.

As Runty traveled far away from familiar haunts and into the strangeness of where he had never set foot before, he was full of wonder. Endless corridors of trees, with sturdy, graceful trunks, lifted their crowns a hundred feet above his head. The wind made the canopy of living green ripple like jade waves tossing their spray to the sky. Runty was more alive than ever: those shining blackberry eyes saw every detail on his journey. Even when ten thousand branches closed in on his world, his eyes found one shining shaft of sunlight amidst the dark forest. It shone on a tree of red and gold, stretching its spray of leaves in gracious gesture toward him. Each leaf poised, trembling slightly, alive at the center of its own breathing. Each one inhaling the same heavy, sweet air by day. Each feeling the cold rush of star-frosted air by night. Each refreshed by the same rain from heaven. Each drooping in the noonday heat. Each sensing, feeling, expanding, and reacting through every pore. Each feeling the same breathless noon, the same opalescent evenfall, when the whole forest turns amethyst for a brief magic moment. Each touched and blessed by the cold starry night, by the brief steaming dawn, when the mist would reluctantly draw back to the sky, and the Colopus Monkeys would hurl on the limb and howl their joy at the morn.

The Jungle

*A*t last, Runty dropped down through the trees on the slopes of Mount Kenya. The cloud-wrapped forest changed to jungle. Birches and conifers gave way to bamboo and silk-cotton trees. Their giant roots sprang from the moist soil and air-breathing parasites lingered everywhere. Saw-leafed ferns snuggled securely in their soggy niches where branches met trunk and orchid flowers sprang out on slender stems upon the open air like great magic night-blooming moths. The air became steamy. Forest animals gave way to jungle inhabitants.

None of them noticed little Runty as he silently slipped between the round, smooth bowls under the feathery emerald and amber canopy of bamboo.

The stone-gray elephants crashed through canes, tearing the trees apart with their ivory tusks and strong trunks. Some of the elephants fed with half-closed eyes, feeling with their trunks rather than seeing with their eyes, their enormous ears swaying rhythmically to the rumbling of their contented stomachs. The great python with its splendid chocolate markings, its pale, yellow eyes that seemed to see nothing yet saw everything, its head equipped with heat sensors that led it deadly and accurately to its warm-blooded prey. Its scaly body seemed to go on and on miraculously as it glided effortlessly, all ribs working smoothly as it slithered through the tangle. The clever baboons eating fruit greedily in the treetop, bending and swaying the topmost branches with their great weight, comically spitting the pits down upon the head of Runty as he journeyed beneath them on the forest floor. Even the crocodiles, their ungainly bodies, lying like bumpy logs, half-submerged in streams that Runty passed over, their protruding, merciless eyes following his every move.

None of these creatures bothered little Runty as he explored and reveled in the great African jungle.

The Bongo

*I*n the hush of midday, Runty spied a bongo, silent and most remote of all the jungle creatures—the elusive antelope. This bongo, a pregnant female, was resting quietly and chewing her cud in the deep green shadows of the enormous, spreading leaves of elephant-ear plants. The narrow, cream stripes on her chestnut-colored body— like slashes of sunlight—naturally concealed her

presence in this perfect camouflage.

But not from little Runty's shining eyes

of curiosity. His gaze went everywhere.

From animal to reptile to insect to the

fishes in the sea. From tree to moth.

From flower to fern. Runty was alive in

wonder and every breath full of love for

all he encountered.

The Encounter

*E*ach new day melded gently into the next as Runty's adventure of love and wonder continued.

One hot, misty dawn, Runty paused at the edge of a glade, watching the golden shafts of new sunlight burst through the banana fronds and lacy bamboo—the night's airy traces dispelling as if by magic as the swirling veils of mist lifted from the jungle and disappeared, slowly into the day. Suddenly, as the mist was clearing, he came face-to-face with a full-grown leopard. Standing there, gazing upon him, frozen in the moment, the leopard did not take his eyes off of Runty.

Because Runty knew only love, he did not run or hide. Instead, he crouched down quietly, tucking his paws under him, looking up at the leopard, enjoying the awesome beauty of the great, wild cat. "What a lovely creature you are," he thought, as he examined the incredibly beautiful rosette patterns on his tawny pelt as soft as silk. There were no waves of fear from Runty, no panic, just a feeling of respectful worship.

Feeling Runty's innocent and harmless energy, the leopard relaxed, his fierceness vanishing. The leopard had never before been openly admired—especially by a creature he could have gobbled in one mouthful. The other smaller creatures had always leapt from him in terror, wanting, naturally, to get as far away as possible from the lethal beauty. "I really don't have to eat him. No, not at all," mused the great cat. Then without a sound and with grace of liquid silk, he slipped across the glade. Runty, quite unselfconsciously, was feeling his own beauty by now. He knew how strong and lithe he was. His world was expanding—his life becoming richer with every passing moment. His heart was full and he silently gave thanks for the creation of such beauty around and within.

Safe in his own radiance of love, the little hyrax got to his feet and continued on his tireless way. Entering the screen of trees, their leaves closing behind him, the entire glade rang silently as he departed.

The Serengeti

*T*he forest gives way to jungle.

The jungle to the grasslands.

And for the first time in his small life, Runty

found himself under the vast expanse of

heaven, facing out over the endless golden

grazing lands of the Serengeti plains that

stretched away before him like a billowing

sea of tawny grasses, uncut, never bruised

by any human, touched only by the hooves

and paws of African beasts.

Gazing out over the sun-dazzled immensity of the Serengeti, Runty's heart wanted to burst with joy. He had never before felt such freedom. He could see all the way to the far horizon. He ran out from under the shade of the last tree behind him, to immerse himself in all he beheld. The hot rays of sun warmed and blessed him. He ran and ran with weightless joy. It was a long while before he slowed to a walk. Then he rolled in the tall wheat-like grasses and stared up at those heavens, stretching his furry little body as wide as it would go. He was filled with absolute bliss.

Runty stayed there for a long time, drifting in and out of a mystical sleep and awake. When evening finally began to arrive, he could look the sun squarely in the face—a red, silken ball poised on the edge of the world. He watched, entranced, as it slowly slipped down between the purple veils that painted the distant horizon. A smoldering ember that disappeared over the golden sea. And the prairie, palpitating with light and heat all that long day, sighed in relief as shadows of evening raced over the land, as if an angel, transfixed all day, had broken the spell, and silently folded its great wings at the approach of night.

As the night crept in, the moon appeared a splendid, silver fingernail caught on the inky black sky of heaven's dusty sleeve. Nearby, shining with a steady light was the planet Venus—the evening star. Then, one by one, all of the stars appeared, and Runty was dazzled, reeling, head tipped back toward the sky, staring at these diamonds scattered across the great dark span by some unseen hand. The Milky Way stood out as a broad river of platinum, spanning the heavens. Not once did

Runty feel lonely. The stars were like thousands of loving eyes, tenderly watching over him, benevolently guarding and cherishing him—a curled ball of clean, warm fur, his cold wet nose deeply buried in a nest of fragrant grasses.

The star-pricked sky, with great dignity above the new moon, remained constant, its focal point, Runty's tiny heart beating in a gentle rhythm. His limbs relaxed in the deep repose of sleep with a smile of love upon his face.

The Peaceable Kingdom

Every day there were fresh wonders on the plains near and far. Runty discovered he was not alone. A party of giant gazelles galloped past—Thomson's gazelles and Impala—their cloven hooves beating the ground like thunder. Clouds of dust, glinting like gold, rose in the still, warm air. The wildebeest and hartebeest, less and greater kudu, the proud oryx, bearing its magnificent horns like curved scimitars, bushbuck, and the long-necked, graceful gerenuk—all presented themselves at one time or another to Runty's worshipful gaze.

Suddenly a large herd of zebras spied Runty and bolted. For one precious, unforgettable moment a living wall of fat, striped rumps with flicking tails thundered by him. In the heat of high noon, under the shade of a thorn tree, lay that greatest of all antelopes, the eland. He was placidly chewing his cud like a barnyard cow. But the leap of this antelope is far from cow-like. A full-grown, slithering cobra suddenly parted the grasses in front of the resting beast. The great, dignified antelope rose in the air as effortlessly and gracefully as the lightest gazelle and made high, wide leaps away from the dangerous snake. Then he found another tree and simply settled back into his pondering meditation, chewing his cud and whiling away the heat of the day on the Serengeti.

The day continued and Runty wandered further along the plains. In the distance, he saw what looked like tall stick-like trees. As he came closer he realized they were not trees at all. They were giraffes! Great placid creatures with twenty-five pound hearts beating, pumping life-giving blood all the way up their long necks to the top of their heads. They were chewing their exclusive diet of thorns, which do not hurt their mouths as they nibble away with their leather-lined lips. They gazed way down upon the fuzzy, furry little rodent as he approached while continuing to tend to the business of eating their thorns. Runty watched in amazement, these exotic cloud-wreathed creatures that were not at all alarmed at this small creature on the ground, so far beneath their all-knowing gaze.

Runty's lineage has been around a very long time. Eons ago when tyrannosaurus rex and other dinosaurs roamed the plains, and centuries later the mastodon and saber-toothed tiger, the hyrax's forbearers played and scampered around these earth-shaking, mighty beasts when their shuddering roars filled the skies, sending terror into every heart. Many species were unable to survive in the evolving pageant. But the hyrax—that rabbit-like rodent, the ancestors of Runty, so small, lightweight, and compact—continued on. One wonders if this small mammal's unusual ability to look straight up into the sky may have been his salvation—straight up into the sky where dreams live and hope thrives and love abides.

The Birds

*T*here were storks everywhere.
Storks who had built nests in
European steeples had come to the African
veldt for winter. Runty saw the lopsided nest
of the hammerhead stork. He is the smallest
of the species but builds the biggest nest. This
nest was sharing uneasy proximity with a
resting leopard who was lying out stretched
on a smooth limb, its distended belly sagging,
all four legs hanging limp on either side.

The powerful feline had dragged his slain antelope to his resting spot. Its remains hung on a lower limb, out of reach by other predators.

Nearby stood a marabou stork—perched, immobile—looking like a judge in his solemn observance. A secretary bird searching for serpents ran swiftly and powerfully over the dry grasses on long, sturdy legs. Like the ostrich, it seemed to be built more for running over the earth. One could hardly imagine it flying through the air, any more than an ostrich.

There were voracious guinea fowl scratching the earth for dropped seeds just like any domestic chicken. And the miracle of a shed feather, perfectly round with white polka dots on a black background. The top of the feathers oiled for shedding rain. The bottom, fluffy for warmth next to the skin.   A hawk perched high on the bare limb of a dead tree. The advancing elephants had long ago torn out the tree's bowels. Elephants had no concern for the trees they killed while filling their bellies. But even if the gentle giant, the elephant, destroys a whole forest, the forest then turns to grassland, extending the prairie, giving more grazing room to plant-eating animals. And many of the trees destroyed by elephants were softened by the presence of weaverbirds' nests, hanging like Christmas tree ornaments from the bare limbs.

Looking up again, Runty saw satiated, bareheaded vultures draped across tree limbs above. They had their fill of the antelope carcass that a few hours earlier, at predawn, had been torn apart by the lioness, her black-maned mate, and family of cubs. They had their fill and left the rest for the taking. After the vultures came the spotted hyenas and the silver-backed jackals, then the bare-necked vultures, fighting over the remains. Then, at the end of these feastings, the wild dogs would saunter in to drag away bones and suck the dry marrow and contentedly chew. Last to eat were the ants.

The African veldt takes care of its own in perfect harmony.

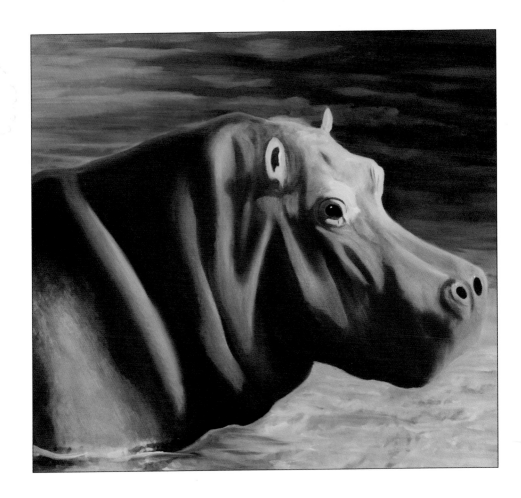

The Hippo

A band of seven proud cranes came to drink on the shore of a pond at twilight before settling down in their beds of fragrant grasses for the night. These grand birds were fascinated by Runty. They the crowned cranes, their large, heavy bodies encased in a gown of iridescent blue feathers with broad-bands and blue-and-white wings. Each bird had a perfect regal circle of feathered spikes crowning the top of its head. Every approach to the pond was exposed and bare. There were a thousand imprints in the mud of cloven hooves and tug marks and claw scratches of the countless animals and birds who had come to drink the resuscitating waters, where, for millennia their vigor had been restored.

Then Runty noticed one shape looming up on the bare, expansive shore. At first he thought it was a big, gray, water-worn rock.   But then a dab of fiery red caught his eye. It was the red, inflamed eye of a hippo, standing motionless at the side of the pond. He was caught in the last light of day. Runty looked longer at the gray beast and noticed there were bloody gashes along its flank. The hippo had been wounded by repeated attacks from the jagged, pro-truding, lower canines of his rival male hippo. Flies swarmed, unrelenting around his body.
Suddenly, a half dozen female hippos emerged from the center of the still pond, their ears and snouts

breaking water. They formed a ring around the triumphant male as if to beg for their own freedom. They ignored the mortally wounded hippo on the shore. He would no longer go by night with his cumbersome comrades like quiet ghosts in the moonlight to graze on grasses as far away as five miles from the pond. He would not live to see the dawn of a new day. The wounded hippo, suffering desperately in silence, was destined to be surrounded that very night by a motley gang of iron-jawed, death-dealing hyenas. The end would come swiftly as it always does on the veldt.

He would proudly take his last stand, separate from the tribe. And as his last sun set over Africa, he would lay down in acceptance of the perfect symmetry on the Serengeti.

The Lammergeyer

Runty tilted his head way back, raised his face to the sky, and looked straight up. A trick that four-legged animals can rarely perform. There, a mile high in the limitless wash of sun-heated air, against the intense eye-smarting blue, was a tiny black dot. Runty didn't know it, but he had spied a lammergeyer, or lamb-snatcher: the undisputed king of all the African vultures. Of all earth's hawks, eagles, and vultures, none other can fly as high or as far as this magnificent carnivorous bird of East Africa. His only cousin is the condor of the Americas. The lammergeyer is brown above and tawny beneath. He grows up to have a ten-foot wingspan. The black-and-white stripes on his head and his eagle like features are characterized by a feathered face, curved beak, fierce eyes, and his long curved claws.

He ranges Central Asia, East Africa, and pockets of Spain, just as the condor ranges the South American

Andes with one isolated pocket in the rocky vastness of the Suspy River Canyon in southern California in the northern hemisphere. This particular lammergeyer had started out that morning early from his nest in the Sudan, had passed over eastern Ethiopia, and then on massive wings had swept the many miles south to the Serengeti plains of Tanzania, having covered Kenya in three hours. Most of his traveling was spent soaring. These enormous wings, with control windows between his spread and sensitized, wing-tipped feathers, are especially adapted to ride upon the updrafts of heated air rising from that great reflector earth below. This enables him to cover vast distances almost effortlessly.

From the earth, he appears a pinprick in the sky. This vantage point allows the lammergeyer's gaze to see all that moves below: the plateau of the central highlands, the vast span of the Serengeti plains, the extinct eroded bowl of the Ngorongoro Crater, and the long, deep Rift Valley to the east. They all stand out like a tiny relief map beneath him. Nothing still or moving escapes those telescopic eyes.

Far below, Runty crouched in the dry grass. An elephant had stumbled, numbed with pain, and had at last fallen. A slow victim of a poisoned arrow tip shot from a native hunter's blowgun. The stricken elephant had wandered in a pain-wrapped daze for weeks, while the powerful kirawi poison on the arrow tip slowly worked its way through that great body to bring it finally to an ignoble crash on the earthen floor, never to rise again. The maddening sense of pain was at last stilled. The eyes dimmed over. The spirit fled. The other elephants in the herd, loyal to their fallen comrade, tried in vain to raise that monolithic body with their trunks and tusks. Saddened, they finally wandered off, reluctantly leaving the carcass to the relentless gaze from a mile above it in the blue. One day, in the distant future, they would return to their comrade's place of bones and pay their respects. Elephants never forget their families.

On target, the bearded vulture starts his magnificent approach. Leaning against the updraft, his ten-foot wingspan outspread, he descends through the thousands of vertical feet of rising sun-heated air in great, wide coils, ever lower, wings outspread, motionless, soundless, the tips of his window-feathers curled upwards toward the all-embracing sun.

Still with his face up, Runty gazed at that awesome descent. Entranced. With that great black shadow sweeping over them, the lesser vultures on the carcass moved aside to make room for this supreme authority. Landing with a springy thud, the lammergeyer folds his great black, sun-glossed wings with perfect care. With measured tread, he strolls to the carcass. The smaller, bareheaded vultures stand about in huddled groups like compliant attendants in the sovereign's court. Even the startled hyenas and silver-backed jackals on the periphery give him room, terrified of that knife-edge of his hooked beak.

The bare head and neck are important to the lesser vultures. The bare skin picks up less bacteria from the sun-rotting carcass. Naturally, the bird goes first for the eyes, a moist, tender delicacy. Then, even as carnivorous animals do, they desire the soft, tender, vital organs inside the dying flesh before they will attack the meat. But not the lammergeyer. His neck and long chin bristles, followed by his whole body, quickly disappeared completely inside the rotting body of the elephant. This posed no threat to the health of the great bird. The powerful rays of the all-cleansing sun would soon dry that feathered head and beard as he returns to his soaring a mile above the earth.

Runty, unnoticed, staggered in awe of the great heavy bird and the majesty of his mile-high, spiraling descent through the sun-bruised, air . Even on the ground, his unchallenged sway over the lesser vultures made them part ranks and retreat to give him the room his kingly presence demanded.

This was an encounter and a memory that Runty would forever hold supreme!

The Flamingo

Runty passed a flamingo standing alone on the plain, miles from any lake in any direction. It was such a sad sight—this lone, pink phantom drooping on the earth. Flamingos fly in flocks, high and fast, on moonlit nights from one shallow feeding lake to another. At night, the air is heavier to better support their bodies. Not just any lake will do. These secret, night-embraced flights often are not even to lakes nearer or more convenient to the lake they've left. They are sometimes many miles from one another, like lake Natron and lake Nakuru are in Kenya. All lakes where they feed must be teeming with the diet of a flamingo; mainly, the delectable, little, rosy freshwater shrimp that, when eaten, give the flamingo feathers their ethereal pink.

The swift flight of the flamingo becomes an endurance test, weeding out all but the most fit. When a flamingo is off its speed or slightly weaker than the rest, too young or too old, is injured or faulting in any way, he simply cannot keep up with his speeding peers on their rigorous flight. Exhausted, he drifts down from high up in the moonlight skies like some lovely, pink petal in its terminal journey from the bough. And there he droops on alien soil, far from water, alone with what comfort he can derive from his private flamingo gods. He is patient with a superb grace. His certain fate will be merciful in its swiftness on the veldt: with foxes, hyenas, and warthogs, baboons, mongoose, and jack-als on the prowl, he won't have long to wait.

The Watering Hole

*A*t the water hole, Runty slaked his thirst, sharing the precious, muddy liquid with the tiny dik-dik, smallest of all the antelope, its inch-long horns like ebony pricks, its agile body the size of a jack rabbit, leaping nervously aside on long, stilt-like legs. While they drank, a stone-gray puff adder sunned on a rock. Later that afternoon, with the sunlight gilding everything with antique gold, Runty watched as the king of the plains, a black-maned lion, drank his fill. His hind legs were erect and his back sloped down to his massive lowered front, leaning on his elbows—forward limbs on the ground at the water's edge. The lion lapped steadily for a long unhurried interlude, afraid of nothing in his entire domain. Then the lioness appeared. He stopped his deliberate drinking to follow her. She slowed. Water still dripping from the corners of his mouth, he caught up with her. She rolled over on her back in the golden dust, raising all four of her immense paws like some common tabby cat.   They rested.

Lions sleep anywhere, flinging their great

bodies down upon the veldt. For who shall

stir a sleeping lion?

In the dry river bottom, a herd of cape

buffalo lowered their sleek, dew-lapped

heads with the great drooping ears and the

down-swept horns, one on either side, to

stare at Runty as he passed. They, too, had

seen hyraxes and so remained unconcerned

as he journeyed onward.

He passed a dragon-like monitor lizard

with its scaly hide gleaming like buffered

bronze in the all-pervading sunlight. He was looking for bird's eggs, flicking in and out his long, blue-black, forked tongue, which was so heavy that it sagged from his jaws.

By now, Runty was familiar with many of the creatures of the plains. He was familiar with the sun and its dependable peak by day. With the lit stars by night. With all that had at first seemed so incomprehensible to Runty. How the moon of such incomparable dignity rose to the vault of the black sky and slowly sank again, tracing an invisible arc on the pathless void all night long with unerring accuracy. Runty marveled at all the faces of this bewitched globe, known from his many nights upon the plains. So many times he had seen how the moon swelled from a curved platinum sliver to its full radiant, dazzling brilliance that paled the stars. And then again the same silver curve, returning to enchant Runty just the way it had on his first night on the African veldt.

The Kopjes

*N*othing escaped the all-seeing, all-loving eyes of Runty. He even became familiar with the kopjes, the rock outcroppings of fantastic shapes at the top of every infrequent rise. These could be seen a long ways off and served as landmarks on the otherwise trackless waste. These rocks often provided the only shadows on the unrelieved plains, serving as a Mecca to panting beasts.

Once, as he passed some of these great rocks in the blue shadows of afternoon, he saw a pride of lions on a ledge. All were relaxed. The kill had been good that morning. They were basking away the golden hours with full tummies, in blissful camaraderie. The females licking the upturned faces of their young like sweet tawny flowers in the late day sun.

Another time, a band of wild dogs was on the mound. One male, clothed in his royal colors of yellow and black so ferocious and ruthless when on the hunt, was wagging his tail, gazing at his mate and her litter, sprawled in the welcome shade. A bat-eared fox and his mate lived on that mound but stayed deep in their den while the dogs were on the kopjes.

At the bottom of the massive stone formations, a warthog family trotted by single file. Each of them swinging low their grotesque snout and protruding tusks while holding aloft their comical little tails with wisps of hair on the end like proud banners in the processional. Maybe these tails served as beacons for the young to follow single file behind their parents in the thick dry grasses.

A pair of cheetahs stared from an anthill. Their small, compact heads and large, bony, bodies, with not an ounce of excess of fat, were covered with tan, spotted hides that blended expertly with the grassy background. Down the side of each gorgeous face, with its prominent, piercing eyes, ran a dark, curved line like a tear-line from the inside corner of the eye, around the muzzle, to the mouth. This is the distinguishing feature of the cheetah face. The couple's babies, hidden in a den nearby, looked like fuzzy, domestic kittens, except for these pronounced and fanciful tear lines.

Deep in the termite mound on which the parent cheetahs were positioned, in the dark, secret underground chambers teeming with insect life, was the obscene body of the termite queen mother looming over her hoards of devoted attendants. This complicated egg-laying machine was the shape of an earth-bound airship. A white silk canopy pulsing with the creative process—denting in and out, here and there to show that, indeed, this monstrous thing was living.

The Ostrich

Ostrich nests are arranged in a slight depression on flat and unprotected ground. They not only contain eggs that were laid at different times, but sometimes by different mothers. If a female ostrich has an egg in her and comes upon a momentarily exposed nest, seeing the nest will trigger the egg-laying instinct and she will leave her egg there among the others.

Except for nest sitting, ostriches are constantly on the move. The baby birds—six-inch miniatures of their parents—come out of the egg equipped to run nearly as fast as their mature parents. All babies must hatch together because they have to immediately travel with a parent bird. Surprisingly, all the eggs in the clutch, although laid at different times and sometimes by different mothers, will hatch together. This is accomplished by a simple and miraculous adaptive process. The first eggs laid lie dormant in the shell until the last egg in the clutch matures. When the youngest baby taps the inside of his shell with his beak, this is the signal that communicates with all the other unborn babies. Then they all tap their shells and break out at once.

"It's time!"

Born together. Miraculous!

Far off from the eminence of a kopje, through the shimmering haze of the Serengeti plains in dry season, Runty could spy movement. It was an ostrich showing off for his female, flapping his soft, curled black-and-white wing feathers, dancing, bowing and dipping before her in the age-old, silent ritual of ostrich courtship. If he were successful, both parents would then take turns sitting on the clutch of the largest eggs on earth.

The Attack

*R*unty traveled across the plains on his nimble, tireless little feet, guided only by the love that beat in his heart.

On the last day of his journey he came across the great gunmetal shape of a huge bull rhinoceros. It loomed up in front of him. The rhino had been engaged in a territorial clash and was now goaded to desperation by flies that were feasting and laying eggs on his open sores. In deep exasperation, the monolithic creature was seeking any moving target on which to vent his spleen. And now, suddenly spying Runty, he zeroed in. The immense head was lowered. The sharp, up-curved horns on his grotesque snout pointed straight at the innocent furry Runty who stood in front of him. Two small monkeys sensed drama. They rushed up the slender trunk of a dew-lit palm, huddled together and began to shiver violently. Then the rhinoceros charged. With no advance warning, those thudding feet were bringing down a thousand pounds of meat and gristle, headed for Runty. The ground trembled and smoked. Light billowed and tore apart like silk on the points of his inescapable horns. The air turned purple. Runty did not move. He was not afraid. Instead, in the last split second and with the noxious breath of the monster fanning his face, the little self-contained mammal stepped expertly aside. The ungainly rhino, a self-propelled missile, thundered past like a runaway locomotive, snorting and steaming through the thorn trees, and vanished.

The monkeys in the palm stopped shivering. Their fright turned to admiration as they saw what appeared a miracle before their round, bulging eyes. The ground stopped smoking. The air stopped billowing.

Everything returned to normal. Insect sounds again rang out from the dry, bent grasses. And Runty, his heart not skipping a beat, continued on his joyous, light-hearted way.

The Sea

*T*he plains, which seemed to have no ending, at last had been crossed. Running up and over the last rise—more sand than earth now—to his immense surprise and delight, Runty found himself on the shore of a calm and azure expanse of sea—the Indian Ocean.

Enraptured, Runty stopped upon the brink. He could not have imagined that the earth, the African plains, serene and mighty, could hold to its bosom such a limitless amount of water.

That it would not fly off into space. He dipped

his forepaws into the cool waters. He crouched

and touched it with his lips. Small, balanced

islands covered with scrub and a few stunted

palms sat in the shallows. Now the tide was at

the ebb, and through the still, transparent water

between the pale fingers of coral reaching for

the light, Runty could clearly see to the white

sandy bottom. A mollusk slid slowly across the

bottom on its foot of flesh, embraced by the

warm seawater.

Runty raised his eyes and gazed out across

the ocean. Neither sail nor man marred the unbroken blue. Only a leaping fish briefly etched its curve of burnished silver before lapsing again into its native element. Runty, his brave little heart knowing no boundary, waded out over the soft white sand bottom between the branches of coral until he was submerged to his shoulders in the crystal water.

The Big Friend

Runty stood transfixed while the delicious new sensation soaked his fur and permeated his every pore. While he exulted there, up to his shoulders in water, a dark shadow slowly glided toward him. Its fin cut the quiet, ebbing surface of the sea. Again, Runty felt no fear. Had the creature come to help him safely across the waters? It was a white-tipped shark that paused to look at him. Because there was no fear or struggle or thrashing around in the waters, the shark sensed Runty's welcome. And in the instant of that pause, without a moment's hesitation, Runty deftly leapt on the shark's back, just in front of the exposed dorsal fin. He clasped the gray, sandpaper hide just behind the gill slits with the firm grip of his delicate forepaws. And the shark glided just below the surface so that Runty could keep his head above the water to breathe.

"Ahhhhhhh." Runty enjoyed the ride. On the shark's back, he saw everything sailing by. Sky, cloud, sea, and even way down beneath the surface of the sea. He loved all

he saw. The laughing, dancing wavelets, each

one reflecting the blue of the sky and conveying

it deep down into the watery depths. Massive

clouds piled on distant opaque thunderheads,

so pure white and gleaming that Runty couldn't

look squarely at them without squinting, his

eyes smarting tears with their dazzlement.

Another great and mobile cloud was directly

overhead. Its purple shadow rested on the sea

like a great sunken island. A great distance off,

the surface of the sea appeared yellow. Upon

approaching, Runty saw there was a coral reef

beneath its white and rosy-tinted fingers that reached through the water for the sun. The shark effortlessly glided across the reef as if flying above a forest. Runty was becoming ecstatic. His whole being knew freedom, fearlessness, and joy. This was the most natural way imaginable for a land mammal to travel over water.

They were accompanied everywhere by a silver-and-black-striped remora, the shark's inescapable companion. Sometimes the remora swam freely under that great, protected blue-white belly, feeding off scraps that fell from the shark's jaws. At other times, the remora attached himself to the shark's undersides with the suction disks on the top of his flat head – a most adaptable way of hitching rides. This remora—a no-nonsense fellow—was filled with awe at his great companion's little passenger. What seemed to him supernatural was to Runty and the shark, supremely natural.

The Secret

Shoals of tiny fish fled in all directions from that great gray, gliding hulk, moving effortlessly at the top of the sea. Their luminous eyes turned back in wonder at the happy little mammal clinging to the shark's back. Not many creatures, or man himself, is given to know the secret that Runty knew:

Leopard fang cannot bruise, rhino tusk cannot pierce, shark's jaw cannot crush, he who walks the earth in love and joy.

The Glossary

GLOSSARY

ba·boon (ba-*boon or, especially Brit.,* b*uh)* any of various large, terrestrial monkeys of the genus *Papio* and related genera, of Africa and Arabia, having a doglike muzzle, large cheek pouches, and a short tail

bon·go (*bong*-goh) bawng- *noun - plural* **-gos**, (*especially collectively*) a reddish-brown antelope, *Taurotragus eurycerus,* of the forests of tropical Africa, having white stripes and large, spirally twisted horns

chee·tah also che·tah (*che* 'ta_) *noun -* A long-legged, swift-running wild cat (*Acinonyx jubatus)* of Africa and southwest Asia, having tawny, black-spotted fur and nonretractile claws. The cheetah, the fastest animal on land, can run for short distances at about 96 kilometers (60 miles) per hour

crane (kran) *noun -* Any of various large wading birds of the family Gruidae, having a long neck, long legs, and a long bill

cobra *(ko.*bra*) noun -* a poisonous snake found in India and Africa *noun -* venomous Asiatic and African elapid snakes that can expand the skin of the neck into a hood

col·o·bus (kol-*uh*-b*uh*s, k*uh*-loh*) noun - plural* **-bus·es, -bi** -bahy, -bahy] any of several large, slender African monkeys of the genus *Colobus,* lacking thumbs and having long silky fur of black and white (*C. polykomos*), black and reddish-brown (*C. badius*), or olive (*C. verus*): now dwindling

dik-dik (*dik*-dik) *noun -* any antelope of the genus *Madoqua* or *Rhynchotragus,* of eastern and southwestern Africa, growing only to 14 in. (36 cm) high at the shoulder

fla·min·go (fla -*ming* -go) *noun - plural* **fla·min·gos** or **fla·min·goes** Any of several large gregarious wading birds of the family Phoenicopteridae of tropical regions, having reddish or pinkish plumage, long legs, a long flexible neck, and a bill turned downward at the tip. A moderate reddish orange

guinea fowl (*gin*ney fowl) *noun -* any of several African, gallinaceous birds of the subfamily Numidinae, esp. a common species, *Numida meleagris,* that has a bony casque on the head and dark gray plumage spotted with white and that is now domesticated and raised for its flesh and eggs

ham·mer·head stork (*ham*-er-hed *stôrk*) a brown heronlike African bird, *Scopus umbretta,* having the head so crested as to resemble a claw hammer

har·te·beest (*hahr*-**tu**- beest) *noun - pural.* **har·te·beests** or **hartebeest** Any of various large African antelopes of the genus *Alcelaphus,* characterized by a reddish-brown coat and ringed, outward-curving horns*)*

hip·po (*hip*-oh) - *plural Informa for:* a large herbivorous mammal, *Hippopotamus amphibius,* having a thick hairless body, short legs, and a large head and muzzle, found in and near the rivers, lakes, etc., of Africa, and able to remain under water for a considerable time

hyena (hahy-*ee*-nuh) *noun -* a doglike carnivore of the family Hyaenidae, of Africa, southwestern Asia, and south central Asia, having a coarse coat, a sloping back, and large teeth and feeding chiefly on carrion, often in packs
hy·rax (*hahy*-raks) *noun - plural* **-rax·es, -ra·ces** any of several species of small mammals of the order Hyracoidea, of Africa and the Mediterranean region, having short legs, ears, and tail, and hooflike nails on the toes
Also called **dassie, das.**

jack·al (silver-backed) (*jak'*_el) *noun -* Any of several doglike mammals of the genus *Canis* of Africa and southern Asia that are mainly foragers feeding on plants, small animals, and occasionally carrion

Ken·ya (*ken*-yuh) *noun -* a republic in E Africa: member of the Commonwealth of Nations; formerly a British crown colony and protectorate. 28,803,085; 223,478 sq. mi. (578,808 sq. km) *Capital:* Nairobi.

lam·mer·gei·er [*lam*-er-*gahy*-er) *noun -* the largest Eurasian bird of prey, *Gypaëtus barbatus,* ranging in the mountains from southern Europe to China, having a wingspread of 9 to 10 ft. (2.7 to 3 m) and black feathers hanging from below the bill like a mustache

leop·ard (*lep*-erd) *noun -* a large, spotted Asian or African carnivore, *Panthera pardus,* of the cat family, usually tawny with black markings; the Old World panther: all leopard populations are threatened or endangered

Marabou stork [*mahr*-**uh**-**boo** stôrk) any of three large storks of the genus *Leptoptilus,* of Africa or the East Indies, having soft, downy feathers under the wings and tail that are used for making a fur-like trimming for women's hats and garments

mon·goose (*mong*-goos) *noun - plural* **goos·es** a slender, ferretlike carnivore, *Herpestes edwardsi,* of India, that feeds on rodents, birds, and eggs, noted esp. for its ability to kill cobras and other venomous snakes

Mount Ken·ya (*Mawnt ken*-**yuh**) *noun -* an extinct volcano in central Kenya. 17,040 ft. (5194 m)

os·trich (*aw*-strich) *noun -* a large, two-toed, swift-footed flightless bird, *Struthio camelus,* indigenous to Africa and Arabia, domesticated for its plumage: the largest of living birds*)*

py·thon (*pi_*-thon*) noun -* Any of various non-venomous snakes of the family Pythonidae, found chiefly in Asia, Africa, and Australia, that coil around and suffocate their prey. Pythons often attain lengths of 6 meters (20 feet) or more

rem·o·ra (rem -er-*uh) noun -* any of several fishes of the family Echeneididae, having on the top of the head a sucking disk by which they can attach themselves to sharks, turtles, ships, and other moving objects

Ser·en·get·i (ser-uhn-*get*-ee) *noun -* a plain in NW Tanzania, including a major wildlife reserve (Serengeti National Park)

Su·dan (soo-*dan) noun -* a region in N Africa, S of the Sahara and Libyan deserts, extending from the Atlantic to the Red Sea

veldt (velt,felt) *noun -* the open country, bearing grass, bushes, or shrubs, or thinly forested, characteristic of parts of southern Africa

vul·ture (*vuhl*-cher) *noun -* any of several large, primarily carrion-eating Old World birds of prey of the family Accipitridae, often having a naked head and less powerful feet than those of the related hawks and eagles

wart·hog (*Wart*-**hawg**, - **hog**) *noun* - an African wild swine, *Phacochoerus aethiopicus,* having large tusks and warty protuberances on the face

wil·de·beest (*wil*-**duh** —beest*) noun - plural* -**beests,** (*especially collectively*) - **beest** Either of two large African antelopes having a drooping mane and beard, a long tufted tail, and curved horns in both sexes
Also called *gnu*

Cape buffalo (*kayp buff*-**uh-lo**) *noun* - a large black buffalo, *Syncerus caffer,* of southern Africa, having horns that meet at the base forming a helmetlike structure over the forehead

Milky Way (*mil*-**kee way**) *noun* - *Astronomy* the spiral galaxy containing our solar system. With the naked eye it is observed as a faint luminous band stretching across the heavens, composed of approximately a trillion stars, most of which are too distant to be seen individually.

rhino (*ry*-**no**) *noun* - massive powerful herbivorous odd-toed ungulate of southeast Asia and Africa having very thick skin and one or two horns on the snout [syn: <u>rhinoceros</u>]

Rift Valley (*rift val*-lee) *noun* - a subsea chasm extending along the crest of a mid-ocean ridge, locus of the magma upwellings that accompany seafloor spreading.

Thomson's gazelle (*tom*-**sens ga**-*zell*) *noun* - a medium-sized antelope, *Gazella thomsoni,* abundant on the grassy steppes and dry bush of the East African plains